The Mysterious Key
and What it Opened

The Mysterious Key and What it Opened

Louisa May Alcott

MINT EDITIONS

The Mysterious Key and What it Opened was first published in 1867.

This edition published by Mint Editions 2020.

ISBN 9781513280080 | E-ISBN 9781513285108

Published by Mint Editions®

MINT
EDITIONS

minteditionbooks.com

Publishing Director: Jennifer Newens
Design & Production: Rachel Lopez Metzger
Project Manager: Micaela Clark
Typesetting: Westchester Publishing Services

Contents

I

THE PROPHECY

Trevlyn lands and Trevlyn gold,
Heir nor heiress e'er shall hold,
Undisturbed, till, spite of rust,
Truth is found in Trevlyn dust.

This is the third time I've found you poring over that old rhyme. What is the charm, Richard? Not its poetry I fancy." And the young wife laid a slender hand on the yellow, time-worn page where, in Old English text, appeared the lines she laughed at.

Richard Trevlyn looked up with a smile and threw by the book, as if annoyed at being discovered reading it. Drawing his wife's hand through his own, he led her back to her couch, folded the soft shawls about her, and, sitting in a low chair beside her, said in a cheerful tone, though his eyes betrayed some hidden care, "My love, that book is a history of our family for centuries, and that old prophecy has never yet been fulfilled, except the 'heir and heiress' line. I am the last Trevlyn, and as the time draws near when my child shall be born, I naturally think of his future, and hope he will enjoy his heritage in peace."

"God grant it!" softly echoed Lady Trevlyn, adding, with a look askance at the old book, "I read that history once, and fancied it must be a romance, such dreadful things are recorded in it. Is it all true, Richard?"

"Yes, dear. I wish it was not. Ours has been a wild, unhappy race till the last generation or two. The stormy nature came in with old Sir Ralph, the fierce Norman knight, who killed his only son in a fit of wrath, by a blow with his steel gauntlet, because the boy's strong will would not yield to his."

"Yes, I remember, and his daughter Clotilde held the castle during a siege, and married her cousin, Count Hugo. 'Tis a warlike race, and I like it in spite of the mad deeds."

"Married her cousin! That has been the bane of our family in times past. Being too proud to mate elsewhere, we have kept to ourselves till idiots and lunatics began to appear. My father was the first who broke the law among us, and I followed his example: choosing the freshest, sturdiest flower I could find to transplant into our exhausted soil."

"I hope it will do you honor by blossoming bravely. I never forget that you took me from a very humble home, and have made me the happiest wife in England."

"And I never forget that you, a girl of eighteen, consented to leave your hills and come to cheer the long-deserted house of an old man like me," returned her husband fondly.

"Nay, don't call yourself old, Richard; you are only forty-five, the boldest, handsomest man in Warwickshire. But lately you look worried; what is it? Tell me, and let me advise or comfort you."

"It is nothing, Alice, except my natural anxiety for you—Well, Kingston, what do you want?"

Trevlyn's tender tones grew sharp as he addressed the entering servant, and the smile on his lips vanished, leaving them dry and white as he glanced at the card he handed him. An instant he stood staring at it, then asked, "Is the man here?"

"In the library, sir."

"I'll come."

Flinging the card into the fire, he watched it turn to ashes before he spoke, with averted eyes: "Only some annoying business, love; I shall soon be with you again. Lie and rest till I come."

With a hasty caress he left her, but as he passed a mirror, his wife saw an expression of intense excitement in his face. She said nothing, and lay motionless for several minutes evidently struggling with some strong impulse.

"He is ill and anxious, but hides it from me; I have a right to know, and he'll forgive me when I prove that it does no harm."

As she spoke to herself she rose, glided noiselessly through the hall, entered a small closet built in the thickness of the wall, and, bending to the keyhole of a narrow door, listened with a half-smile on her lips at the trespass she was committing. A murmur of voices met her ear. Her husband spoke oftenest, and suddenly some word of his dashed the smile from her face as if with a blow. She started, shrank, and shivered, bending lower with set teeth, white cheeks, and panic-stricken heart. Paler and paler grew her lips, wilder and wilder her eyes, fainter and fainter her breath, till, with a long sigh, a vain effort to save herself, she sank prone upon the threshold of the door, as if struck down by death.

"Mercy on us, my lady, are you ill?" cried Hester, the maid, as her mistress glided into the room looking like a ghost, half an hour later.

"I am faint and cold. Help me to my bed, but do not disturb Sir Richard."

A shiver crept over her as she spoke, and, casting a wild, woeful look about her, she laid her head upon the pillow like one who never cared to lift it up again. Hester, a sharp-eyed, middle-aged woman, watched the pale creature for a moment, then left the room muttering, "Something is wrong, and Sir Richard must know it. That black-bearded man came for no good, I'll warrant."

At the door of the library she paused. No sound of voices came from within; a stifled groan was all she heard; and without waiting to knock she went in, fearing she knew not what. Sir Richard sat at his writing table pen in hand, but his face was hidden on his arm, and his whole attitude betrayed the presence of some overwhelming despair.

"Please, sir, my lady is ill. Shall I send for anyone?"

No answer. Hester repeated her words, but Sir Richard never stirred. Much alarmed, the woman raised his head, saw that he was unconscious, and rang for help. But Richard Trevlyn was past help, though he lingered for some hours. He spoke but once, murmuring faintly, "Will Alice come to say good-bye?"

"Bring her if she can come," said the physician.

Hester went, found her mistress lying as she left her, like a figure carved in stone. When she gave the message, Lady Trevlyn answered sternly, "Tell him I will not come," and turned her face to the wall, with an expression which daunted the woman too much for another word.

Hester whispered the hard answer to the physician, fearing to utter it aloud, but Sir Richard heard it, and died with a despairing prayer for pardon on his lips.

When day dawned Sir Richard lay in his shroud and his little daughter in her cradle, the one unwept, the other unwelcomed by the wife and mother, who, twelve hours before, had called herself the happiest woman in England. They thought her dying, and at her own command gave her the sealed letter bearing her address which her husband left behind him. She read it, laid it in her bosom, and, waking from the trance which seemed to have so strongly chilled and changed her, besought those about her with passionate earnestness to save her life.

For two days she hovered on the brink of the grave, and nothing but the indomitable will to live saved her, the doctors said. On the third day she rallied wonderfully, and some purpose seemed to gift her with unnatural strength. Evening came, and the house was very still, for all the sad bustle of preparation for Sir Richard's funeral was over, and he lay for the last night under his own roof. Hester sat in the darkened chamber of her mistress, and no sound broke the hush but the low lullaby the nurse was singing to the fatherless baby in the adjoining room. Lady Trevlyn seemed to sleep, but suddenly put back the curtain, saying abruptly, "Where does he lie?"

"In the state chamber, my lady," replied Hester, anxiously watching the feverish glitter of her mistress's eye, the flush on her cheek, and the unnatural calmness of her manner.

"Help me to go there; I must see him."

"It would be your death, my lady. I beseech you, don't think of it," began the woman; but Lady Trevlyn seemed not to hear her, and something in the stern pallor of her face awed the woman into submission.

Wrapping the slight form of her mistress in a warm cloak, Hester half-led, half-carried her to the state room, and left her on the threshold.

"I must go in alone; fear nothing, but wait for me here," she said, and closed the door behind her.

Five minutes had not elapsed when she reappeared with no sign of grief on her rigid face.

"Take me to my bed and bring my jewel box," she said, with a shuddering sigh, as the faithful servant received her with an exclamation of thankfulness.

When her orders had been obeyed, she drew from her bosom the portrait of Sir Richard which she always wore, and, removing the ivory oval from the gold case, she locked the former in a tiny drawer of the casket, replaced the empty locket in her breast, and bade Hester give the jewels to Watson, her lawyer, who would see them put in a safe place till the child was grown.

"Dear heart, my lady, you'll wear them yet, for you're too young to grieve all your days, even for so good a man as my blessed master. Take comfort, and cheer up, for the dear child's sake if no more."

"I shall never wear them again" was all the answer as Lady Trevlyn drew the curtains, as if to shut out hope.

Sir Richard was buried and, the nine days' gossip over, the mystery of his death died for want of food, for the only person who could have explained it was in a state which forbade all allusion to that tragic day.

For a year Lady Trevlyn's reason was in danger. A long fever left her so weak in mind and body that there was little hope of recovery, and her days were passed in a state of apathy sad to witness. She seemed to have forgotten everything, even the shock which had so sorely stricken her. The sight of her child failed to rouse her, and month after month slipped by, leaving no trace of their passage on her mind, and but slightly renovating her feeble body.

Who the stranger was, what his aim in coming, or why he never reappeared, no one discovered. The contents of the letter left by Sir Richard were unknown, for the paper had been destroyed by Lady Trevlyn and no clue could be got from her. Sir Richard had died of heart disease, the physicians said, though he might have lived years had no sudden shock assailed him. There were few relatives to make investigations, and friends soon forgot the sad young widow; so the years rolled on, and Lillian the heiress grew from infancy to childhood in the shadow of this mystery.

II

Paul

"C ome, child, the dew is falling, and it is time we went in."

"No, no, Mamma is not rested yet, so I may run down to the spring if I like." And Lillian, as willful as winsome, vanished among the tall ferns where deer couched and rabbits hid.

Hester leisurely followed, looking as unchanged as if a day instead of twelve years had passed since her arms received the little mistress, who now ruled her like a tyrant. She had taken but a few steps when the child came flying back, exclaiming in an excited tone, "Oh, come quick! There's a man there, a dead man. I saw him and I'm frightened!"

"Nonsense, child, it's one of the keepers asleep, or some stroller who has no business here. Take my hand and we'll see who it is."

Somewhat reassured, Lillian led her nurse to one of the old oaks beside the path, and pointed to a figure lying half hidden in the fern. A slender, swarthy boy of sixteen, with curly black hair, dark brows, and thick lashes, a singularly stern mouth, and a general expression of strength and pride, which added character to his boyish face and dignified his poverty. His dress betrayed that, being dusty and threadbare, his shoes much worn, and his possessions contained in the little bundle on which he pillowed his head. He was sleeping like one quite spent with weariness, and never stirred, though Hester bent away the ferns and examined him closely.

"He's not dead, my deary; he's asleep, poor lad, worn out with his day's tramp, I dare say." "I'm glad he's alive, and I wish he'd wake up. He's a pretty boy, isn't he? See what nice hands he's got, and his hair is more curly than mine. Make him open his eyes, Hester," commanded the little lady, whose fear had given place to interest.

"Hush, he's stirring. I wonder how he got in, and what he wants," whispered Hester.

"I'll ask him," and before her nurse could arrest her, Lillian drew a tall fern softly over the sleeper's face, laughing aloud as she did so.

The boy woke at the sound, and without stirring lay looking up at the lovely little face bent over him, as if still in a dream.

"*Bella cara*," he said, in a musical voice. Then, as the child drew back abashed at the glance of his large, bright eyes, he seemed to wake entirely and, springing to his feet, looked at Hester with a quick, searching glance. Something in his face and air caused the woman to soften her tone a little, as she said gravely, "Did you wish to see any one at the Hall?"

"Yes. Is Lady Trevlyn here?" was the boy's answer, as he stood cap in hand, with the smile fading already from his face.

"She is, but unless your business is very urgent you had better see Parks, the keeper; we don't trouble my lady with trifles."

"I've a note for her from Colonel Daventry; and as it is *not* a trifle, I'll deliver it myself, if you please."

Hester hesitated an instant, but Lillian cried out, "Mamma is close by, come and see her," and led the way, beckoning as she ran.

The lad followed with a composed air, and Hester brought up the rear, taking notes as she went with a woman's keen eye.

Lady Trevlyn, a beautiful, pale woman, delicate in health and melancholy in spirit, sat on a rustic seat with a book in her hand; not reading, but musing with an absent mind. As the child approached, she held out her hand to welcome her, but neither smiled nor spoke.

"Mamma, here is a—a person to see you," cried Lillian, rather at a loss how to designate the stranger, whose height and gravity now awed her.

"A note from Colonel Daventry, my lady," and with a bow the boy delivered the missive.

Scarcely glancing at him, she opened it and read:

My Dear Friend,

The bearer of this, Paul Jex, has been with me some months and has served me well. I brought him from Paris, but he is English born, and, though friendless, prefers to remain here, even after we leave, as we do in a week. When I last saw you you mentioned wanting a lad to help in the garden; Paul is accustomed to that employment, though my wife used him as a sort of page in the house. Hoping you may be able to give him shelter, I venture to send him. He is honest, capable, and trustworthy in all respects. Pray try him, and oblige,

Yours sincerely,
J. R. Daventry

"The place is still vacant, and I shall be very glad to give it to you, if you incline to take it," said Lady Trevlyn, lifting her eyes from the note and scanning the boy's face.

"I do, madam," he answered respectfully.

"The colonel says you are English," added the lady, in a tone of surprise.

The boy smiled, showing a faultless set of teeth, as he replied, "I am, my lady, though just now I may not look it, being much tanned and very dusty. My father was an Englishman, but I've lived abroad a good deal since he died, and got foreign ways, perhaps."

As he spoke without any accent, and looked full in her face with a pair of honest blue eyes under the dark lashes, Lady Trevlyn's momentary doubt vanished.

"Your age, Paul?"

"Sixteen, my lady."

"You understand gardening?"

"Yes, my lady."

"And what else?"

"I can break horses, serve at table, do errands, read aloud, ride after a young lady as groom, illuminate on parchment, train flowers, and make myself useful in any way."

The tone, half modest, half eager, in which the boy spoke, as well as the odd list of his accomplishments, brought a smile to Lady Trevlyn's lips, and the general air of the lad prepossessed her.

"I want Lillian to ride soon, and Roger is rather old for an escort to such a little horsewoman. Don't you think we might try Paul?" she said, turning to Hester.

The woman gravely eyed the lad from head to foot, and shook her head, but an imploring little gesture and a glance of the handsome eyes softened her heart in spite of herself.

"Yes, my lady, if he does well about the place, and Parks thinks he's steady enough, we might try it by-and-by."

Lillian clapped her hands and, drawing nearer, exclaimed confidingly, as she looked up at her new groom, "I know he'll do, Mamma. I like him very much, and I hope you'll let him train my pony for me. Will you, Paul?"

"Yes."

As he spoke very low and hastily, the boy looked away from the eager little face before him, and a sudden flush of color crossed his dark cheek.

Hester saw it and said within herself, "That boy has good blood in his veins. He's no clodhopper's son, I can tell by his hands and feet, his air and walk. Poor lad, it's hard for him, I'll warrant, but he's not too proud for honest work, and I like that."

"You may stay, Paul, and we will try you for a month. Hester, take him to Parks and see that he is made comfortable. Tomorrow we will see what he can do. Come, darling, I am rested now."

As she spoke, Lady Trevlyn dismissed the boy with a gracious gesture and led her little daughter away. Paul stood watching her, as if forgetful of his companion, till she said, rather tartly, "Young man, you'd better have thanked my lady while she was here than stare after her now it's too late. If you want to see Parks, you'd best come, for I'm going."

"Is that the family tomb yonder, where you found me asleep?" was the unexpected reply to her speech, as the boy quietly followed her, not at all daunted by her manner.

"Yes, and that reminds me to ask how you got in, and why you were napping there, instead of doing your errand properly?"

"I leaped the fence and stopped to rest before presenting myself, Miss Hester" was the cool answer, accompanied by a short laugh as he confessed his trespass.

"You look as if you'd had a long walk; where are you from?"

"London."

"Bless the boy! It's fifty miles away."

"So my shoes show; but it's a pleasant trip in summer time."

"But why did you walk, child! Had you no money?"

"Plenty, but not for wasting on coaches, when my own stout legs could carry me. I took a two days' holiday and saved my money for better things."

"I like that," said Hester, with an approving nod. "You'll get on, my lad, if that's your way, and I'll lend a hand, for laziness is my abomination, and one sees plenty nowadays."

"Thank you. That's friendly, and I'll prove that I am grateful. Please tell me, is my lady ill?"

"Always delicate since Sir Richard died."

"How long ago was that?"

"Ten years or more."

"Are there no young gentlemen in the family?"

"No, Miss Lillian is an only child, and a sweet one, bless her!"

"A proud little lady, I should say."

"And well she may be, for there's no better blood in England than the Trevlyns, and she's heiress to a noble fortune."

"Is that the Trevlyn coat of arms?" asked the boy abruptly, pointing to a stone falcon with the motto ME AND MINE carved over the gate through which they were passing.

"Yes. Why do you ask?"

"Mere curiosity; I know something of heraldry and often paint these things for my own pleasure. One learns odd amusements abroad," he added, seeing an expression of surprise on the woman's face.

"You'll have little time for such matters here. Come in and report yourself to the keeper, and if you'll take my advice ask no questions of him, for you'll get no answers."

"I seldom ask questions of men, as they are not fond of gossip." And the boy nodded with a smile of mischievous significance as he entered the keeper's lodge.

A sharp lad and a saucy, if he likes. I'll keep my eye on him, for my lady takes no more thought of such things than a child, and Lillian cares for nothing but her own will. He has a taking way with him, though, and knows how to flatter. It's well he does, poor lad, for life's a hard matter to a friendless soul like him.

As she thought these thoughts Hester went on to the house, leaving Paul to win the good graces of the keeper, which he speedily did by assuming an utterly different manner from that he had worn with the woman.

That night, when the boy was alone in his own room, he wrote a long letter in Italian describing the events of the day, enclosed a sketch of the falcon and motto, directed it to "Father Cosmo Carmela, Genoa," and lay down to sleep, muttering, with a grim look and a heavy sigh, "So far so well; I'll not let my heart be softened by pity, or my purpose change till my promise is kept. Pretty child, I wish I had never seen her!"

III

SECRET SERVICE

In a week Paul was a favorite with the household; even prudent Hester felt the charm of his presence, and owned that Lillian was happier for a young companion in her walks. Hitherto the child had led a solitary life, with no playmates of her own age, such being the will of my lady; therefore she welcomed Paul as a new and delightful amusement, considering him her private property and soon transferring his duties from the garden to the house. Satisfied of his merits, my lady yielded to Lillian's demands, and Paul was installed as page to the young lady. Always respectful and obedient, he never forgot his place, yet seemed unconsciously to influence all who approached him, and win the goodwill of everyone.

My lady showed unusual interest in the lad, and Lillian openly displayed her admiration for his accomplishments and her affection for her devoted young servitor. Hester was much flattered by the confidence he reposed in her, for to her alone did he tell his story, and of her alone asked advice and comfort in his various small straits. It was as she suspected: Paul was a gentleman's son, but misfortune had robbed him of home, friends, and parents, and thrown him upon the world to shift for himself. This sad story touched the woman's heart, and the boy's manly spirit won respect. She had lost a son years ago, and her empty heart yearned over the motherless lad. Ashamed to confess the tender feeling, she wore her usual severe manner to him in public, but in private softened wonderfully and enjoyed the boy's regard heartily.

"Paul, come in. I want to speak with you a moment," said my lady, from the long window of the library to the boy who was training vines outside.

Dropping his tools and pulling off his hat, Paul obeyed, looking a little anxious, for the month of trial expired that day. Lady Trevlyn saw and answered the look with a gracious smile.

"Have no fears. You are to stay if you will, for Lillian is happy and I am satisfied with you."

"Thank you, my lady." And an odd glance of mingled pride and pain shone in the boy's downcast eyes.

"That is settled, then. Now let me say what I called you in for. You spoke of being able to illuminate on parchment. Can you restore this old book for me?"

She put into his hand the ancient volume Sir Richard had been reading the day he died. It had lain neglected in a damp nook for years till my lady discovered it, and, sad as were the associations connected with it, she desired to preserve it for the sake of the weird prophecy if nothing else. Paul examined it, and as he turned it to and fro in his hands it opened at the page oftenest read by its late master. His eye kindled as he looked, and with a quick gesture he turned as if toward the light, in truth to hide the flash of triumph that passed across his face. Carefully controlling his voice, he answered in a moment, as he looked up, quite composed, "Yes, my lady, I can retouch the faded colors on these margins and darken the pale ink of the Old English text. I like the work, and will gladly do it if you like."

"Do it, then, but be very careful of the book while in your hands. Provide what is needful, and name your own price for the work," said his mistress.

"Nay, my lady, I am already paid—"

"How so?" she asked, surprised.

Paul had spoken hastily, and for an instant looked embarrassed, but answered with a sudden flush on his dark cheeks, "You have been kind to me, and I am glad to show my, gratitude in any way, my lady."

"Let that pass, my boy. Do this little service for me and we will see about the recompense afterward." And with a smile Lady Trevlyn left him to begin his work.

The moment the door closed behind her a total change passed over Paul. He shook his clenched hand after her with a gesture of menace, then tossed up the old book and caught it with an exclamation of delight, as he reopened it at the worn page and reread the inexplicable verse.

"Another proof, another proof! The work goes bravely on, Father Cosmo; and boy as I am, I'll keep my word in spite of everything," he muttered.

"What is that you'll keep, lad?" said a voice behind him.

"I'll keep my word to my lady, and do my best to restore this book, Mrs. Hester," he answered, quickly recovering himself.

"Ah, that's the last book poor Master read. I hid it away, but my lady found it in spite of me," said Hester, with a doleful sigh.

"Did he die suddenly, then?" asked the boy.

"Dear heart, yes; I found him dying in this room with the ink scarce dry on the letter he left for my lady. A mysterious business and a sad one."

"Tell me about it. I like sad stories, and I already feel as if I belonged to the family, a loyal retainer as in the old times. While you dust the books and I rub the mold off this old cover, tell me the tale, please, Mrs. Hester."

She shook her head, but yielded to the persuasive look and tone of the boy, telling the story more fully than she intended, for she loved talking and had come to regard Paul as her own, almost.

"And the letter? What was in it?" asked the boy, as she paused at the catastrophe.

"No one ever knew but my lady."

"She destroyed it, then?"

"I thought so, till a long time afterward, one of the lawyers came pestering me with questions, and made me ask her. She was ill at the time, but answered with a look I shall never forget, 'No, it's not burnt, but no one shall ever see it.' I dared ask no more, but I fancy she has it safe somewhere and if it's ever needed she'll bring it out. It was only some private matters, I fancy."

"And the stranger?"

"Oh, he vanished as oddly as he came, and has never been found. A strange story, lad. Keep silent, and let it rest."

"No fear of my tattling," and the boy smiled curiously to himself as he bent over the book, polishing the brassbound cover.

"What are you doing with that pretty white wax?" asked Lillian the next day, as she came upon Paul in a quiet corner of the garden and found him absorbed in some mysterious occupation.

With a quick gesture he destroyed his work, and, banishing a momentary expression of annoyance, he answered in his accustomed tone as he began to work anew, "I am molding a little deer for you, Miss Lillian. See, here is a rabbit already done, and I'll soon have a stag also."

"It's very pretty! How many nice things you can do, and how kind you are to think of my liking something new. Was this wax what you went to get this morning when you rode away so early?" asked the child.

"Yes, Miss Lillian. I was ordered to exercise your pony and I made him useful as well. Would you like to try this? It's very easy."

Lillian was charmed, and for several days wax modeling was her favorite play. Then she tired of it, and Paul invented a new amusement, smiling his inexplicable smile as he threw away the broken toys of wax.

"You are getting pale and thin, keeping such late hours, Paul. Go to bed, boy, go to bed, and get your sleep early," said Hester a week afterward, with a motherly air, as Paul passed her one morning.

"And how do you know I don't go to bed?" he asked, wheeling about.

"My lady has been restless lately, and I sit up with her till she sleeps. As I go to my room, I see your lamp burning, and last night I got as far as your door, meaning to speak to you, but didn't, thinking you'd take it amiss. But really you are the worse for late hours, child."

"I shall soon finish restoring the book, and then I'll sleep. I hope I don't disturb you. I have to grind my colors, and often make more noise than I mean to."

Paul fixed his eyes sharply on the woman as he spoke, but she seemed unconscious of it, and turned to go on, saying indifferently, "Oh, that's the odd sound, is it? No, it doesn't trouble me, so grind away, and make an end of it as soon as may be."

An anxious fold in the boy's forehead smoothed itself away as he left her, saying to himself with a sigh of relief, "A narrow escape; it's well I keep the door locked."

The boy's light burned no more after that, and Hester was content till a new worry came to trouble her. On her way to her room late one night, she saw a tall shadow flit down one of the side corridors that branched from the main one. For a moment she was startled, but, being a woman of courage, she followed noiselessly, till the shadow seemed to vanish in the gloom of the great hall.

"If the house ever owned a ghost I'd say that's it, but it never did, so I suspect some deviltry. I'll step to Paul. He's not asleep, I dare say. He's a brave and a sensible lad, and with him I'll quietly search the house."

Away she went, more nervous than she would own, and tapped at the boy's door. No one answered, and, seeing that it was ajar, Hester whisked in so hurriedly that her candle went out. With an impatient exclamation at her carelessness she glided to the bed, drew the curtain, and put forth her hand to touch the sleeper. The bed was empty. A disagreeable thrill shot through her, as she assured herself of the fact by groping along the narrow bed. Standing in the shadow of the curtain, she stared about the dusky room, in which objects were visible by the light of a new moon.

"Lord bless me, what is the boy about! I do believe it was him I saw in the—" She got no further in her mental exclamation for the sound of light approaching footsteps neared her. Slipping around the bed she waited in the shadow, and a moment after Paul appeared, looking pale and ghostly, with dark, disheveled hair, wide-open eyes, and a cloak thrown over his shoulders. Without a pause he flung it off, laid himself in bed, and seemed to sleep at once.

"Paul! Paul!" whispered Hester, shaking him, after a pause of astonishment at the whole proceeding.

"Hey, what is it?" And he sat up, looking drowsily about him.

"Come, come, no tricks, boy. What are you doing, trailing about the house at this hour and in such trim?"

"Why, Hester, is it you?" he exclaimed with a laugh, as he shook off her grip and looked up at her in surprise.

"Yes, and well it is me. If it had been any of those silly girls, the house would have been roused by this time. What mischief is afoot that you leave your bed and play ghost in this wild fashion?"

"Leave my bed! Why, my good soul, I haven't stirred, but have been dreaming with all my might these two hours. What do you mean, Hester?"

She told him as she relit her lamp, and stood eyeing him sharply the while. When she finished he was silent a minute, then said, looking half vexed and half ashamed, "I see how it is, and I'm glad you alone have found me out. I walk in my sleep sometimes, Hester, that's the truth. I thought I'd got over it, but it's come back, you see, and I'm sorry for it. Don't be troubled. I never do any mischief or come to any harm. I just take a quiet promenade and march back to bed again. Did I frighten you?"

"Just a trifle, but it's nothing. Poor lad, you'll have to have a bedfellow or be locked up; it's dangerous to go roaming about in this way," said Hester anxiously.

"It won't last long, for I'll get more tired and then I shall sleep sounder. Don't tell anyone, please, else they'll laugh at me, and that's not pleasant. I don't mind your knowing for you seem almost like a mother, and I thank you for it with all my heart."

He held out his hand with the look that was irresistible to Hester. Remembering only that he was a motherless boy, she stroked the curly hair off his forehead, and kissed him, with the thought of her own son warm at her heart.

"Good night, dear. I'll say nothing, but give you something that will ensure quiet sleep hereafter."

With that she left him, but would have been annoyed could she have seen the convulsion of boyish merriment which took possession of him when alone, for he laughed till the tears ran down his cheeks.

IV

Vanished

He's a handsome lad, and one any woman might be proud to call her son," said Hester to Bedford, the stately butler, as they lingered at the hall door one autumn morning to watch their young lady's departure on her daily ride.

"You are right, Mrs. Hester, he's a fine lad, and yet he seems above his place, though he does look the very picture of a lady's groom," replied Bedford approvingly.

So he did, as he stood holding the white pony of his little mistress, for the boy gave an air to whatever he wore and looked like a gentleman even in his livery. The dark-blue coat with silver buttons, the silver band about his hat, his white-topped boots and bright spurs, spotless gloves, and tightly drawn belt were all in perfect order, all becoming, and his handsome, dark face caused many a susceptible maid to blush and simper as they passed him. "Gentleman Paul," as the servants called him, was rather lofty and reserved among his mates, but they liked him nonetheless, for Hester had dropped hints of his story and quite a little romance had sprung up about him. He stood leaning against the docile creature, sunk in thought, and quite unconscious of the watchers and whisperers close by. But as Lillian appeared he woke up, attended to his duties like a well-trained groom, and lingered over his task as if he liked it. Down the avenue he rode behind her, but as they turned into a shady lane Lillian beckoned, saying, in the imperious tone habitual to her, "Ride near me. I wish to talk."

Paul obeyed, and amused her with the chat she liked till they reached a hazel copse; here he drew rein, and, leaping down, gathered a handful of ripe nuts for her.

"How nice. Let us rest a minute here, and while I eat a few, please pull some of those flowers for Mamma. She likes a wild nosegay better than any I can bring her from the garden."

Lillian ate her nuts till Paul came to her with a hatful of late flowers and, standing by her, held the impromptu basket while she made up a bouquet to suit her taste.

"You shall have a posy, too; I like you to wear one in your buttonhole as the ladies' grooms do in the Park," said the child, settling a scarlet poppy in the blue coat.

"Thanks, Miss Lillian, I'll wear your colors with all my heart, especially today, for it is my birthday." And Paul looked up at the blooming little face with unusual softness in his keen blue eyes.

"Is it? Why, then, you're seventeen; almost a man, aren't you?"

"Yes, thank heaven," muttered the boy, half to himself.

"I wish I was as old. I shan't be in my teens till autumn. I must give you something, Paul, because I like you very much, and you are always doing kind things for me. What shall it be?" And the child held out her hand with a cordial look and gesture that touched the boy.

With one of the foreign fashions which sometimes appeared when he forgot himself, he kissed the small hand, saying impulsively, "My dear little mistress, I want nothing but your goodwill—and your forgiveness," he added, under his breath.

"You have that already, Paul, and I shall find something to add to it. But what is that?" And she laid hold of a little locket which had slipped into sight as Paul bent forward in his salute.

He thrust it back, coloring so deeply that the child observed it, and exclaimed, with a mischievous laugh, "It is your sweetheart, Paul. I heard Bessy, my maid, tell Hester she was sure you had one because you took no notice of them. Let me see it. Is she pretty?"

"Very pretty," answered the boy, without showing the picture.

"Do you like her very much?" questioned Lillian, getting interested in the little romance.

"Very much," and Paul's black eyelashes fell.

"Would you die for her, as they say in the old songs?" asked the girl, melodramatically.

"Yes, Miss Lillian, or live for her, which is harder."

"Dear me, how very nice it must be to have anyone care for one so much," said the child innocently. "I wonder if anybody ever will for me?"

> *"Love comes to all soon or late,*
> *And maketh gay or sad;*
> *For every bird will find its mate,*
> *And every lass a lad,"*

sang Paul, quoting one of Hester's songs, and looking relieved that Lillian's thoughts had strayed from him. But he was mistaken.

"Shall you marry this sweetheart of yours someday?" asked Lillian, turning to him with a curious yet wistful look.

"Perhaps."

"You look as if there was no 'perhaps' about it," said the child, quick to read the kindling of the eye and the change in the voice that accompanied the boy's reply.

"She is very young and I must wait, and while I wait many things may happen to part us."

"Is she a lady?"

"Yes, a wellborn, lovely little lady, and I'll marry her if I live." Paul spoke with a look of decision, and a proud lift of the head that contrasted curiously with the badge of servitude he wore.

Lillian felt this, and asked, with a sudden shyness coming over her, "But you are a gentleman, and so no one will mind even if you are not rich."

"How do you know what I am?" he asked quickly.

"I heard Hester tell the housekeeper that you were not what you seemed, and one day she hoped you'd get your right place again. I asked Mamma about it, and she said she would not let me be with you so much if you were not a fit companion for me. I was not to speak of it, but she means to be your friend and help you by-and-by."

"Does she?"

And the boy laughed an odd, short laugh that jarred on Lillian's ear and made her say reprovingly, "You are proud, I know, but you'll let us help you because we like to do it, and I have no brother to share my money with."

"Would you like one, or a sister?" asked Paul, looking straight into her face with his piercing eyes.

"Yes, indeed! I long for someone to be with me and love me, as Mamma can't."

"Would you be willing to share everything with another person— perhaps have to give them a great many things you like and now have all to yourself?"

"I think I should. I'm selfish, I know, because everyone pets and spoils me, but if I loved a person dearly I'd give up anything to them. Indeed I would, Paul, pray believe me."

She spoke earnestly, and leaned on his shoulder as if to enforce her words. The boy's arm stole around the little figure in the saddle, and a beautiful bright smile broke over his face as he answered warmly, "I do believe it, dear, and it makes me happy to hear you say so. Don't be afraid, I'm your equal, but I'll not forget that you are my little mistress till I can change from groom to gentleman."

He added the last sentence as he withdrew his arm, for Lillian had shrunk a little and blushed with surprise, not anger, at this first breach of respect on the part of her companion. Both were silent for a moment, Paul looking down and Lillian busy with her nosegay. She spoke first, assuming an air of satisfaction as she surveyed her work.

"That will please Mamma, I'm sure, and make her quite forget my naughty prank of yesterday. Do you know I offended her dreadfully by peeping into the gold case she wears on her neck? She was asleep and I was sitting by her. In her sleep she pulled it out and said something about a letter and Papa. I wanted to see Papa's face, for I never did, because the big picture of him is gone from the gallery where the others are, so I peeped into the case when she let it drop and was so disappointed to find nothing but a key."

"A key! What sort of a key?" cried Paul in an eager tone.

"Oh, a little silver one like the key of my piano, or the black cabinet. She woke and was very angry to find me meddling."

"What did it belong to?" asked Paul.

"Her treasure box, she said, but I don't know where or what that is, and I dare not ask any more, for she forbade my speaking to her about it. Poor Mamma! I'm always troubling her in some way or other."

With a penitent sigh, Lillian tied up her flowers and handed them to Paul to carry. As she did so, the change in his face struck her.

"How grim and old you look," she exclaimed. "Have I said anything that troubles you?"

"No, Miss Lillian. I'm only thinking."

"Then I wish you wouldn't think, for you get a great wrinkle in your forehead, your eyes grow almost black, and your mouth looks fierce. You are a very odd person, Paul; one minute as gay as any boy, and the next as grave and stern as a man with a deal of work to do."

"I *have* got a deal of work to do, so no wonder I look old and grim."

"What work, Paul?"

"To make my fortune and win my lady."

When Paul spoke in that tone and wore that look, Lillian felt as if they had changed places, and he was the master and she the servant.

She wondered over this in her childish mind, but proud and willful as she was, she liked it, and obeyed him with unusual meekness when he suggested that it was time to return. As he rode silently beside her, she stole covert glances at him from under her wide hat brim, and studied his unconscious face as she had never done before. His lips moved now and then but uttered no audible sound, his black brows were knit, and once his hand went to his breast as if he thought of the little sweetheart whose picture lay there.

He's got a trouble. I wish he'd tell me and let me help him if I can. I'll make him show me that miniature someday, for I'm interested in that girl, thought Lillian with a pensive sigh.

As he held his hand for her little foot in dismounting her at the hall door, Paul seemed to have shaken off his grave mood, for he looked up and smiled at her with his blithest expression. But Lillian appeared to be the thoughtful one now and with an air of dignity, very pretty and becoming, thanked her young squire in a stately manner and swept into the house, looking tall and womanly in her flowing skirts.

Paul laughed as he glanced after her and, flinging himself onto his horse, rode away to the stables at a reckless pace, as if to work off some emotion for which he could find no other vent.

"Here's a letter for you, lad, all the way from some place in Italy. Who do you know there?" said Bedford, as the boy came back.

With a hasty "Thank you," Paul caught the letter and darted away to his own room, there to tear it open and, after reading a single line, to drop into a chair as if he had received a sudden blow. Growing paler and paler he read on, and when the letter fell from his hands he exclaimed, in a tone of despair, "How could he die at such a time!"

For an hour the boy sat thinking intently, with locked door, curtained window, and several papers strewn before him. Letters, memoranda, plans, drawings, and bits of parchment, all of which he took from a small locked portfolio always worn about him. Over these he pored with a face in which hope, despondency, resolve, and regret alternated rapidly. Taking the locket out he examined a ring which lay in one side, and the childish face which smiled on him from the other. His eyes filled as he locked and put it by, saying tenderly, "Dear little heart! I'll not forget or desert her whatever happens. Time must help me, and to time I must leave my work. One more attempt and then I'm off."

"I'll go to bed now, Hester; but while you get my things ready I'll take a turn in the corridor. The air will refresh me."

As she spoke, Lady Trevlyn drew her wrapper about her and paced softly down the long hall lighted only by fitful gleams of moonlight and the ruddy glow of the fire. At the far end was the state chamber, never used now, and never visited except by Hester, who occasionally went in to dust and air it, and my lady, who always passed the anniversary of Sir Richard's death alone there. The gallery was very dark, and she seldom went farther than the last window in her restless walks, but as she now approached she was startled to see a streak of yellow light under the door. She kept the key herself and neither she nor Hester had been there that day. A cold shiver passed over her for, as she looked, the shadow of a foot darkened the light for a moment and vanished as if someone had noiselessly passed. Obeying a sudden impulse, my lady sprang forward and tried to open the door. It was locked, but as her hand turned the silver knob a sound as if a drawer softly closed met her ear. She stooped to the keyhole but it was dark, a key evidently being in the lock. She drew back and flew to her room, snatched the key from her dressing table, and, bidding Hester follow, returned to the hall.

"What is it, my lady?" cried the woman, alarmed at the agitation of her mistress.

"A light, a sound, a shadow in the state chamber. Come quick!" cried Lady Trevlyn, adding, as she pointed to the door, "There, there, the light shines underneath. Do you see it?"

"No, my lady, it's dark," returned Hester.

It was, but never pausing my lady thrust in the key, and to her surprise it turned, the door flew open, and the dim, still room was before them. Hester boldly entered, and while her mistress slowly followed, she searched the room, looking behind the tall screen by the hearth, up the wide chimney, in the great wardrobe, and under the ebony cabinet, where all the relics of Sir Richard were kept. Nothing appeared, not even a mouse, and Hester turned to my lady with an air of relief. But her mistress pointed to the bed shrouded in dark velvet hangings, and whispered breathlessly, "You forgot to look there."

Hester had not forgotten, but in spite of her courage and good sense she shrank a little from looking at the spot where she had last seen her master's dead face. She believed the light and sound to be phantoms of my lady's distempered fancy, and searched merely to satisfy her. The mystery of Sir Richard's death still haunted the minds of all who remembered it, and even Hester felt a superstitious dread of that room. With a nervous laugh she looked under the bed and, drawing back the heavy curtains, said soothingly, "You see, my lady, there's nothing there."

But the words died on her lips, for, as the pale glimmer of the candle pierced the gloom of that funeral couch, both saw a face upon the pillow: a pale face framed in dark hair and beard, with closed eyes and the stony look the dead wear. A loud, long shriek that roused the house broke from Lady Trevlyn as she fell senseless at the bedside, and dropping both curtain and candle Hester caught up her mistress and fled from the haunted room, locking the door behind her.

In a moment a dozen servants were about them, and into their astonished ears Hester poured her story while vainly trying to restore her lady. Great was the dismay and intense the unwillingness of anyone to obey when Hester ordered the men to search the room again, for she was the first to regain her self-possession.

"Where's Paul? He's the heart of a man, boy though he is," she said angrily as the men hung back.

"He's not here. Lord! Maybe it was him a-playing tricks, though it ain't like him," cried Bessy, Lillian's little maid.

"No, it can't be him, for I locked him in myself. He walks in his sleep sometimes, and I was afraid he'd startle my lady. Let him sleep; this would only excite him and set him to marching again. Follow me, Bedford and James, I'm not afraid of ghosts or rogues."

With a face that belied her words Hester led the way to the awful room, and flinging back the curtain resolutely looked in. The bed was empty, but on the pillow was plainly visible the mark of a head and a single scarlet stain, as of blood. At that sight Hester turned pale and caught the butler's arm, whispering with a shudder, "Do you remember the night we put him in his coffin, the drop of blood that fell from his white lips? Sir Richard has been here."

"Good Lord, ma'am, don't say that! We can never rest in our beds if such things are to happen," gasped Bedford, backing to the door.

"It's no use to look, we've found all we shall find so go your ways and tell no one of this," said the woman in a gloomy tone, and, having assured herself that the windows were fast, Hester locked the room and ordered everyone but Bedford and the housekeeper to bed. "Do you sit outside my lady's door till morning," she said to the butler, "and you,

Mrs. Price, help me to tend my poor lady, for if I'm not mistaken this night's work will bring on the old trouble."

Morning came, and with it a new alarm; for, though his door was fast locked and no foothold for even a sparrow outside the window, Paul's room was empty, and the boy nowhere to be found.

V

A Hero

Four years had passed, and Lillian was fast blooming into a lovely woman: proud and willful as ever, but very charming, and already a belle in the little world where she still reigned a queen. Owing to her mother's ill health, she was allowed more freedom than is usually permitted to an English girl of her age; and, during the season, often went into company with a friend of Lady Trevlyn's who was chaperoning two young daughters of her own. To the world Lillian seemed a gay, free-hearted girl; and no one, not even her mother, knew how well she remembered and how much she missed the lost Paul. No tidings of him had ever come, and no trace of him was found after his flight. Nothing was missed, he went without his wages, and no reason could be divined for his departure except the foreign letter. Bedford remembered it, but forgot what postmark it bore, for he had only been able to decipher "Italy." My lady made many inquiries and often spoke of him; but when month after month passed and no news came, she gave him up, and on Lillian's account feigned to forget him. Contrary to Hester's fear, she did not seem the worse for the nocturnal fright, but evidently connected the strange visitor with Paul, or, after a day or two of nervous exhaustion, returned to her usual state of health. Hester had her own misgivings, but, being forbidden to allude to the subject, she held her peace, after emphatically declaring that Paul would yet appear to set her mind at rest.

"Lillian, Lillian, I've such news for you! Come and hear a charming little romance, and prepare to see the hero of it!" cried Maud Churchill, rushing into her friend's pretty boudoir one day in the height of the season.

Lillian lay on a couch, rather languid after a ball, and listlessly begged Maud to tell her story, for she was dying to be amused.

"Well my, dear, just listen and you'll be as enthusiastic as I am," cried Maud. And throwing her bonnet on one chair, her parasol on another, and her gloves anywhere, she settled herself on the couch and began: "You remember reading in the papers, some time ago, that fine account of the young man who took part in the Italian revolution and did that heroic thing with the bombshell?"

"Yes, what of him?" asked Lillian, sitting up.

"He is my hero, and we are to see him tonight."

"Go on, go on! Tell all, and tell it quickly," she cried.

"You know the officers were sitting somewhere, holding a council, while the city (I forget the name) was being bombarded, and how a shell came into the midst of them, how they sat paralyzed, expecting it to burst, and how this young man caught it up and ran out with it, risking his own life to save theirs?"

"Yes, yes, I remember!" And Lillian's listless face kindled at the recollection.

"Well, an Englishman who was there was so charmed by the act that, finding the young man was poor and an orphan, he adopted him. Mr. Talbot was old, and lonely, and rich, and when he died, a year after, he left his name and fortune to this Paolo."

"I'm glad, I'm glad!" cried Lillian, clapping her hands with a joyful face. "How romantic and charming it is!"

"Isn't it? But, my dear creature, the most romantic part is to come. Young Talbot served in the war, and then came to England to take possession of his property. It's somewhere down in Kent, a fine place and good income, all his; and he deserves it. Mamma heard a deal about him from Mrs. Langdon, who knew old Talbot and has seen the young man. Of course all the girls are wild to behold him, for he is very handsome and accomplished, and a gentleman by birth. But the dreadful part is that he is already betrothed to a lovely Greek girl, who came over at the same time, and is living in London with a companion; quite elegantly, Mrs. Langdon says, for she called and was charmed. This girl has been seen by some of our gentlemen friends, and they already rave about the 'fair Helene,' for that's her name."

Here Maud was forced to stop for breath, and Lillian had a chance to question her.

"How old is she?"

"About eighteen or nineteen, they say."

"Very pretty?"

"Ravishing, regularly Greek and divine, Fred Raleigh says."

"When is she to be married?"

"Don't know; when Talbot gets settled, I fancy."

"And he? Is he as charming as she?"

"Quite, I'm told. He's just of age, and is, in appearance as in everything else, a hero of romance."

"How came your mother to secure him for tonight?"

"Mrs. Langdon is dying to make a lion of him, and begged to bring him. He is very indifferent on such things and seems intent on his own affairs. Is grave and old for his years, and doesn't seem to care much for pleasure and admiration, as most men would after a youth like his, for he has had a hard time, I believe. For a wonder, he consented to come when Mrs. Langdon asked him, and I flew off at once to tell you and secure you for tonight."

"A thousand thanks. I meant to rest, for Mamma frets about my being so gay; but she won't object to a quiet evening with you. What shall we wear?" And here the conversation branched off on the all-absorbing topic of dress.

When Lillian joined her friend that evening, the hero had already arrived, and, stepping into a recess, she waited to catch a glimpse of him. Maud was called away, and she was alone when the crowd about the inner room thinned and permitted young Talbot to be seen. Well for Lillian that no one observed her at that moment, for she grew pale and sank into a chair, exclaiming below her breath, "It is Paul—*my Paul!*"

She recognized him instantly, in spite of increased height, a dark moustache, and martial bearing. It was Paul, older, graver, handsomer, but still "her Paul," as she called him, with a flush of pride and delight as she watched him, and felt that of all there she knew him best and loved him most. For the childish affection still existed, and this discovery added a tinge of romance that made it doubly dangerous as well as doubly pleasant.

Will he know me? she thought, glancing at a mirror which reflected a slender figure with bright hair, white arms, and brilliant eyes; a graceful little head, proudly carried, and a sweet mouth, just then very charming, as it smiled till pearly teeth shone between the ruddy lips.

I'm glad I'm not ugly, and I hope he'll like me, she thought, as she smoothed the golden ripples on her forehead, settled her sash, and shook out the folds of her airy dress in a flutter of girlish excitement. "I'll pretend not to know him, when we meet, and see what he will do," she said, with a wicked sense of power; for being forewarned she was forearmed, and, fearing no betrayal of surprise on her own part, was eager to enjoy any of which he might be guilty.

Leaving her nook, she joined a group of young friends and held herself prepared for the meeting. Presently she saw Maud and

Mrs. Langdon approaching, evidently intent on presenting the hero to the heiress.

"Mr. Talbot, Miss Trevlyn," said the lady. And looking up with a well-assumed air of indifference, Lillian returned the gentleman's bow with her eyes fixed full upon his face.

Not a feature of that face changed, and so severely unconscious of any recognition was it that the girl was bewildered. For a moment she fancied she had been mistaken in his identity, and a pang of disappointment troubled her; but as he moved a chair for Maud, she saw on the one ungloved hand a little scar which she remembered well, for he received it in saving her from a dangerous fall. At the sight all the happy past rose before her, and if her telltale eyes had not been averted they would have betrayed her. A sudden flush of maidenly shame dyed her cheek as she remembered that last ride, and the childish confidences then interchanged. This Helen was the little sweetheart whose picture he wore, and now, in spite of all obstacles, he had won both fortune and ladylove. The sound of his voice recalled her thoughts, and glancing up she met the deep eyes fixed on her with the same steady look they used to wear. He had addressed her, but what he said she knew not, beyond a vague idea that it was some slight allusion to the music going on in the next room. With a smile which would serve for an answer to almost any remark, she hastily plunged into conversation with a composure that did her credit in the eyes of her friends, who stood in awe of the young hero, for all were but just out.

"Mr. Talbot hardly needs an introduction here, for his name is well-known among us, though this is perhaps his first visit to England?" she said, flattering herself that this artful speech would entrap him into the reply she wanted.

With a slight frown, as if the allusion to his adventure rather annoyed him, and a smile that puzzled all but Lillian, he answered very simply, "It is not my first visit to this hospitable island. I was here a few years ago, for a short time, and left with regret."

"Then you have old friends here?" And Lillian watched him as she spoke.

"I had. They had doubtless forgotten me now," he said, with a sudden shadow marring the tranquillity of his face.

"Why doubt them? If they were true friends, they will not forget."

The words were uttered impulsively, almost warmly, but Talbot made no response, except a polite inclination and an abrupt change in the conversation.

"That remains to be proved. Do you sing, Miss Trevlyn?"

"A little." And Lillian's tone was both cold and proud.

"A great deal, and very charmingly," added Maud, who took pride in her friend's gifts both of voice and beauty. "Come, dear, there are so few of us you will sing, I know. Mamma desired me to ask you when Edith had done."

To her surprise Lillian complied, and allowed Talbot to lead her to the instrument. Still hoping to win some sign of recognition from him, the girl chose an air he taught her and sang it with a spirit and skill that surprised the listeners who possessed no key to her mood. At the last verse her voice suddenly faltered, but Talbot took up the song and carried her safely through it with his well-tuned voice.

"You know the air then?" she said in a low tone, as a hum of commendation followed the music.

"All Italians sing it, though few do it like yourself," he answered quietly, restoring the fan he had held while standing beside her.

Provoking boy! why won't he know me? thought Lillian. And her tone was almost petulant as she refused to sing again.

Talbot offered his arm and led her to a seat, behind which stood a little statuette of a child holding a fawn by a daisy chain.

"Pretty, isn't it?" she said, as he paused to look at it instead of taking the chair before her. "I used to enjoy modeling tiny deer and hinds in wax, as well as making daisy chains. Is sculpture among the many accomplishments which rumor tells us you possess?"

"No. Those who, like me, have their own fortunes to mold find time for little else," he answered gravely, still examining the marble group.

Lillian broke her fan with an angry flirt, for she was tired of her trial, and wished she had openly greeted him at the beginning; feeling now how pleasant it would have been to sit chatting of old times, while her friends dared hardly address him at all. She was on the point of calling him by his former name, when the remembrance of what he had been arrested the words on her lips. He was proud; would he not dread to have it known that, in his days of adversity, he had been a servant? For if she betrayed her knowledge of his past, she would be forced to tell where and how that knowledge was gained. No, better wait till they met alone, she thought; he would thank her for her delicacy, and she could easily explain her motive. He evidently wished to seem a stranger, for once she caught a gleam of the old, mirthful mischief in his eye, as she glanced up unexpectedly. He did remember her, she was sure, yet was trying her, perhaps, as she tried him. Well, she would stand the test and enjoy the joke by-and-by. With this fancy in her head she assumed a gracious air and chatted away in her most charming style, feeling both gay and excited, so anxious was she to please, and so glad to recover her early friend. A naughty whim seized her as her eye fell on a portfolio of classical engravings which someone had left in disorder on a table near her. Tossing them over she asked his opinion of several, and then handed him one in which Helen of Troy was represented as giving her hand to the irresistible Paris.

"Do you think her worth so much bloodshed, and deserving so much praise?" she asked, vainly trying to conceal the significant smile that would break loose on her lips and sparkle in her eyes.

Talbot laughed the short, boyish laugh so familiar to her ears, as he glanced from the picture to the arch questioner, and answered in a tone that made her heart beat with a nameless pain and pleasure, so full of suppressed ardor was it:

"Yes! 'All for love or the world well lost' is a saying I heartily agree to. La belle Helene is my favorite heroine, and I regard Paris as the most enviable of men."

"I should like to see her."

The wish broke from Lillian involuntarily, and she was too much confused to turn it off by any general expression of interest in the classical lady.

"You may sometime," answered Talbot, with an air of amusement; adding, as if to relieve her, "I have a poetical belief that all the lovely women of history or romance will meet, and know, and love each other in some charming hereafter."

"But I'm no heroine and no beauty, so I shall never enter your poetical paradise," said Lillian, with a pretty affectation of regret.

"Some women are beauties without knowing it, and the heroines of romances never given to the world. I think you and Helen will yet meet, Miss Trevlyn."

As he spoke, Mrs. Langdon beckoned, and he left her pondering over his last words, and conscious of a secret satisfaction in his implied promise that she should see his betrothed.

"How do you like him?" whispered Maud, slipping into the empty chair.

"Very well," was the composed reply; for Lillian enjoyed her little mystery too much to spoil it yet.

"What did you say to him? I longed to hear, for you seemed to enjoy yourselves very much, but I didn't like to be a marplot."

Lillian repeated a part of the conversation, and Maud professed to be consumed with jealousy at the impression her friend had evidently made.

"It is folly to try to win the hero, for he is already won, you know," answered Lillian, shutting the cover on the pictured Helen with a sudden motion as if glad to extinguish her.

"Oh dear, no; Mrs. Langdon just told Mamma that she was mistaken about their being engaged; for she asked him and he shook his head, saying Helen was his ward."

"But that is absurd, for he's only a boy himself. It's very odd, isn't it? Never mind, I shall soon know all about it."

"How?" cried Maud, amazed at Lillian's assured manner.

"Wait a day or two and, I'll tell you a romance in return for yours. Your mother beckons to me, so I know Hester has come. Good night. I've had a charming time."

And with this tantalizing adieu, Lillian slipped away. Hester was waiting in the carriage, but as Lillian appeared, Talbot put aside the footman and handed her in, saying very low, in the well-remembered tone:

"Good night, my little mistress."

VI

Fair Helen

To no one but her mother and Hester did Lillian confide the discovery she had made. None of the former servants but old Bedford remained with them, and till Paul chose to renew the old friendship it was best to remain silent. Great was the surprise and delight of our lady and Hester at the good fortune of their protege, and many the conjectures as to how he would explain his hasty flight.

"You will go and see him, won't you, Mamma, or at least inquire about him?" said Lillian, eager to assure the wanderer of a welcome, for those few words of his had satisfied her entirely.

"No, dear, it is for him to seek us, and till he does, I shall make no sign. He knows where we are, and if he chooses he can renew the acquaintance so strangely broken off. Be patient, and above all things remember, Lillian, that you are no longer a child," replied my lady, rather disturbed by her daughter's enthusiastic praises of Paul.

"I wish I was, for then I might act as I feel, and not be afraid of shocking the proprieties." And Lillian went to bed to dream of her hero.

For three days she stayed at home, expecting Paul, but he did not come, and she went out for her usual ride in the Park, hoping to meet him. An elderly groom now rode behind her, and she surveyed him with extreme disgust, as she remembered the handsome lad who had once filled that place. Nowhere did Paul appear, but in the Ladies' Mile she passed an elegant brougham in which sat a very lovely girl and a mild old lady.

"That is Talbot's fiancee," said Maud Churchill, who had joined her. "Isn't she beautiful?"

"Not at all—yes, very," was Lillian's somewhat peculiar reply, for jealousy and truth had a conflict just then. "He's so perfectly absorbed and devoted that I am sure that story is true, so adieu to our hopes," laughed Maud.

"Did you have any? Good-bye, I must go." And Lillian rode home at a pace which caused the stout groom great distress.

"Mamma, I've seen Paul's betrothed!" she cried, running into her mother's boudoir.

"And I have seen Paul himself," replied my lady, with a warning look, for there he stood, with half-extended hand, as if waiting to be acknowledged.

Lillian forgot her embarrassment in her pleasure, and made him an elaborate curtsy, saying, with a half-merry, half-reproachful glance, "Mr. Talbot is welcome in whatever guise he appears."

"I choose to appear as Paul, then, and offer you a seat, Miss Lillian," he said, assuming as much of his boyish manner as he could.

Lillian took it and tried to feel at ease, but the difference between the lad she remembered and the man she now saw was too great to be forgotten.

"Now tell us your adventures, and why you vanished away so mysteriously four years ago," she said, with a touch of the childish imperiousness in her voice, though her frank eyes fell before his.

"I was about to do so when you appeared with news concerning my cousin," he began.

"Your cousin!" exclaimed Lillian.

"Yes, Helen's mother and my own were sisters. Both married Englishmen, both died young, leaving us to care for each other. We were like a brother and sister, and always together till I left her to serve Colonel Daventry. The death of the old priest to whom I entrusted her recalled me to Genoa, for I was then her only guardian. I meant to have taken leave of you, my lady, properly, but the consequences of that foolish trick of mine frightened me away in the most unmannerly fashion."

"Ah, it was you, then, in the state chamber; I always thought so," and Lady Trevlyn drew a long breath of relief.

"Yes, I heard it whispered among the servants that the room was haunted, and I felt a wish to prove the truth of the story and my own courage. Hester locked me in, for fear of my sleepwalking; but I lowered myself by a rope and then climbed in at the closet window of the state chamber. When you came, my lady, I thought it was Hester, and slipped into the bed, meaning to give her a fright in return for her turning the key on me. But when your cry showed me what I had done, I was filled with remorse, and escaped as quickly and quietly as possible. I should have asked pardon before; I do now, most humbly, my lady, for it was sacrilege to play pranks *there*."

During the first part of his story Paul's manner had been frank and composed, but in telling the latter part, his demeanor underwent a curious change. He fixed his eyes on the ground and spoke as if repeating a lesson, while his color varied, and a half-proud, half-submissive expression replaced the former candid one. Lillian observed this, and it disturbed her, but my lady took it for shame at his boyish freak and received his confession kindly, granting a free pardon and expressing sincere pleasure at his amended fortunes. As he listened, Lillian saw him clench his hand hard and knit his brows, assuming the grim look she had often seen, as if trying to steel himself against some importunate emotion or rebellious thought.

"Yes, half my work is done, and I have a home, thanks to my generous benefactor, and I hope to enjoy it well and wisely," he said in a grave tone, as if the fortune had not yet brought him his heart's desire.

"And when is the other half of the work to be accomplished, Paul? That depends on your cousin, perhaps." And Lady Trevlyn regarded him with a gleam of womanly curiosity in her melancholy eyes.

"It does, but not in the way you fancy, my lady. Whatever Helen may be, she is not my fiancee yet, Miss Lillian." And the shadow lifted as he laughed, looking at the young lady, who was decidedly abashed, in spite of a sense of relief caused by his words.

"I merely accepted the world's report," she said, affecting a nonchalant air.

"The world is a liar, as you will find in time" was his abrupt reply.

"I hope to see this beautiful cousin, Paul. Will she receive us as old friends of yours?"

"Thanks, not yet, my lady. She is still too much a stranger here to enjoy new faces, even kind ones. I have promised perfect rest and freedom for a time, but you shall be the first whom she receives."

Again Lillian detected the secret disquiet which possessed him, and her curiosity was roused. It piqued her that this Helen felt no desire to meet her and chose to seclude herself, as if regardless of the interest and admiration she excited. "I *will* see her in spite of her refusal, for I only caught a glimpse in the Park. Something is wrong, and I'll discover it, for it evidently worries Paul, and perhaps I can help him."

As this purpose sprang up in the warm but willful heart of the girl, she regained her spirits and was her most charming self while the young man stayed. They talked of many things in a pleasant, confidential manner, though when Lillian recalled that hour, she was surprised to find how little Paul had really told them of his past life or future plans. It was agreed among them to say nothing of their former relations, except to old Bedford, who was discretion itself, but to appear to the world as new-made friends—thus avoiding unpleasant and unnecessary explanations which would only excite gossip. My lady asked him to dine, but he had business out of town and declined, taking his leave with a lingering look, which made Lillian steal away to study her face in the mirror and wonder if she looked her best, for in Paul's eyes she had read undisguised admiration.

Lady Trevlyn went to her room to rest, leaving the girl free to ride, drive, or amuse herself as she liked. As if fearing her courage would fail if she delayed, Lillian ordered the carriage, and, bidding Hester mount guard over her, she drove away to St. John's Wood.

"Now, Hester, don't lecture or be prim when I tell you that we are going on a frolic," she began, after getting the old woman into an amiable mood by every winning wile she could devise. "I think you'll like it, and if it's found out I'll take the blame. There is some mystery about Paul's cousin, and I'm going to find it out."

"Bless you, child, how?"

"She lives alone here, is seldom seen, and won't go anywhere or receive anyone. That's not natural in a pretty girl. Paul won't talk about her, and, though he's fond of her, he always looks grave and grim when I ask questions. That's provoking, and I won't hear it. Maud is engaged to Raleigh, you know; well, he confided to her that he and a friend had found out where Helen was, had gone to the next villa, which is empty, and under pretense of looking at it got a peep at the girl in her garden. I'm going to do the same."

"And what am *I* to do?" asked Hester, secretly relishing the prank, for she was dying with curiosity to behold Paul's cousin.

"You are to do the talking with the old woman, and give me a chance to look. Now say you will, and I'll behave myself like an angel in return."

Hester yielded, after a few discreet scruples, and when they reached Laburnum Lodge played her part so well that Lillian soon managed to stray away into one of the upper rooms which overlooked the neighboring garden. Helen was there, and with eager eyes the girl scrutinized her. She was very beautiful, in the classical style; as fair and finely molded as a statue, with magnificent dark hair and eyes, and possessed of that perfect grace which is as effective as beauty. She was alone, and when first seen was bending over a flower which she caressed and seemed to examine with great interest as she stood a long time motionless before it. Then she began to pace slowly around and around the little grass plot, her hands hanging loosely clasped before her, and her eyes fixed on vacancy as if absorbed in thought. But as the first effect of her beauty passed away, Lillian found something peculiar about her. It was not the somewhat foreign dress and ornaments she wore; it was in her face, her movements, and the tone of her voice, for as she walked she sang a low, monotonous song, as if unconsciously. Lillian watched her keenly, marking the aimless motions of the little hands, the apathy of the lovely face, and the mirthless accent of the voice; but most of all the vacant fixture of the great dark eyes. Around and around she went, with an elastic step and a mechanical regularity wearisome to witness.

What is the matter with her? thought Lillian anxiously, as this painful impression increased with every scrutiny of the unconscious girl. So abashed was she that Hester's call was unheard, and Hester was unseen as she came and stood beside her. Both looked a moment, and as they looked an old lady came from the house and led Helen in, still murmuring her monotonous song and moving her hands as if to catch and hold the sunshine.

"Poor dear, poor dear. No wonder Paul turns sad and won't talk of her, and that she don't see anyone," sighed Hester pitifully.

"What is it? I see, but don't understand," whispered Lillian.

"She's an innocent, deary, an idiot, though that's a hard word for a pretty creature like her."

"How terrible! Come away, Hester, and never breathe to anyone what we have seen." And with a shudder and sense of pain and pity lying heavy at her heart, she hurried away, feeling doubly guilty in the discovery of this affliction. The thought of it haunted her continually; the memory of the lonely girl gave her no peace; and a consciousness of deceit burdened her unspeakably, especially in Paul's presence. This lasted for a week, then Lillian resolved to confess, hoping that when he found she knew the truth he would let her share his cross and help to lighten it. Waiting her opportunity, she seized a moment when her mother was absent, and with her usual frankness spoke out impetuously.

"Paul, I've done wrong, and I can have no peace till I am pardoned. I have seen Helen."

"Where, when, and how?" he asked, looking disturbed and yet relieved.

She told him rapidly, and as she ended she looked up at him with her sweet face, so full of pity, shame, and grief it would have been impossible to deny her anything.

"Can you forgive me for discovering this affliction?"

"I think I could forgive you a far greater fault, Lillian," he answered, in a tone that said many things.

"But deceit is so mean, so dishonorable and contemptible, how can you so easily pardon it in me?" she asked, quite overcome by this forgiveness, granted without any reproach.

"Then you would find it hard to pardon such a thing in another?" he said, with the expression that always puzzled her.

"Yes, it would be hard; but in those I loved, I could forgive much for love's sake."

With a sudden gesture he took her hand saying, impulsively, "How little changed you are! Do you remember that last ride of ours nearly five years ago?"

"Yes, Paul," she answered, with averted eyes.

"And what we talked of?"

"A part of that childish gossip I remember well."

"Which part?"

"The pretty little romance you told me." And Lillian looked up now, longing to ask if Helen's childhood had been blighted like her youth.

Paul dropped her hand as if he, read her thoughts, and his own hand went involuntarily toward his breast, betraying that the locket still hung there.

"What did I say?" he asked, smiling at her sudden shyness.

"You vowed you'd win and wed your fair little lady-love if you lived."

"And so I will," he cried, with sudden fire in his eyes.

"What, marry her?"

"Aye, that I will."

"Oh Paul, will you tie yourself for life to a—" The word died on her lips, but a gesture of repugnance finished the speech.

"A what?" he demanded, excitedly.

"An innocent, one bereft of reason," stammered Lillian, entirely forgetting herself in her interest for him.

"Of whom do you speak?" asked Paul, looking utterly bewildered,

"Of poor Helen."

"Good heavens, who told you that base lie?" And his voice deepened with indignant pain.

"I saw her, you did not deny her affliction; Hester said so, and I believed it. Have I wronged her, Paul?"

"Yes, cruelly. She is blind, but no idiot, thank God."

There was such earnestness in his voice, such reproach in his words, and such ardor in his eye, that Lillian's pride gave way, and with a broken entreaty for pardon, she covered up her face, weeping the bitterest tears she ever shed. For in that moment, and the sharp pang it brought her, she felt how much she loved Paul and how hard it was to lose him. The childish affection had blossomed into a woman's passion, and in a few short weeks had passed through many phases of jealousy, hope, despair, and self-delusion. The joy she felt on seeing him again, the pride she took in him, the disgust Helen caused her, the relief she had not dared to own even to herself, when she fancied fate had put an insurmountable barrier between Paul and his cousin, the despair at finding it only a fancy, and the anguish of hearing him declare his unshaken purpose to marry his first love—all these conflicting emotions had led to this hard moment, and now self-control deserted her in her need. In spite of her efforts the passionate tears would have their way, though Paul soothed her with assurances of entire forgiveness, promises of Helen's friendship, and every gentle device he could imagine. She commanded herself at last by a strong effort, murmuring eagerly as she shrank from the hand that put back her fallen hair, and the face so full of tender sympathy bending over her:

"I am so grieved and ashamed at what I have said and done. I shall never dare to see Helen. Forgive me, and forget this folly. I'm sad and heavyhearted just now; it's the anniversary of Papa's death, and Mamma always suffers so much at such times that I get nervous."

"It is your birthday also. I remembered it, and ventured to bring a little token in return for the one you gave me long ago. This is a talisman, and tomorrow I will tell you the legend concerning it. Wear it for my sake, and God bless you, dear."

The last words were whispered hurriedly; Lillian saw the glitter of an antique ring, felt the touch of bearded lips on her hand, and Paul was gone.

But as he left the house he set his teeth, exclaiming low to himself, "Yes, tomorrow there shall be an end of this! We must risk everything and abide the consequences now. I'll have no more torment for any of us."

VII

The Secret Key

"I s Lady Trevlyn at home, Bedford?" asked Paul, as he presented himself at an early hour next day, wearing the keen, stern expression which made him look ten years older than he was.

"No, sir, my lady and Miss Lillian went down to the Hall last night."

"No ill news, I hope?" And the young man's eye kindled as if he felt a crisis at hand.

"Not that I heard, sir. Miss Lillian took one of her sudden whims and would have gone alone, if my lady hadn't given in much against her will, this being a time when she is better away from the place."

"Did they leave no message for me?"

"Yes, sir. Will you step in and read the note at your ease. We are in sad confusion, but this room is in order."

Leading the way to Lillian's boudoir, the man presented the note and retired. A few hasty lines from my lady, regretting the necessity of this abrupt departure, yet giving no reason for it, hoping they might meet next season, but making no allusion to seeing him at the Hall, desiring Lillian's thanks and regards, but closing with no hint of Helen, except compliments. Paul smiled as he threw it into the fire, saying to himself, "Poor lady, she thinks she has escaped the danger by flying, and Lillian tries to hide her trouble from me. Tender little heart! I'll comfort it without delay."

He sat looking about the dainty room still full of tokens of her presence. The piano stood open with a song he liked upon the rack; a bit of embroidery, whose progress he had often watched, lay in her basket with the little thimble near it; there was a strew of papers on the writing table, torn notes, scraps of drawing, and ball cards; a pearl-colored glove lay on the floor; and in the grate the faded flowers he had brought two days before. As his eye roved to and fro, he seemed to enjoy some happy dream, broken too soon by the sound of servants shutting up the house. He arose but lingered near the table, as if longing to search for some forgotten hint of himself.

"No, there has been enough lock picking and stealthy work; I'll do no more for her sake. This theft will harm no one and tell no tales." And snatching up the glove, Paul departed.

LOUISA MAY ALCOTT

"Helen, the time has come. Are you ready?" he asked, entering her room an hour later.

"I am ready." And rising, she stretched her hand to him with a proud expression, contrasting painfully with her helpless gesture.

"They have gone to the Hall, and we must follow. It is useless to wait longer; we gain nothing by it, and the claim must stand on such proof as we have, or fall for want of that one link. I am tired of disguise. I want to be myself and enjoy what I have won, unless I lose it all."

"Paul, whatever happens, remember we cling together and share good or evil fortune as we always have done. I am a burden, but I cannot live without you, for you are my world. Do not desert me."

She groped her way to him and clung to his strong arm as if it was her only stay. Paul drew her close, saying wistfully, as he caressed the beautiful sightless face leaning on his shoulder, "*Mia cara*, would it break your heart, if at the last hour I gave up all and let the word remain unspoken? My courage fails me, and in spite of the hard past I would gladly leave them in peace."

"No, no, you shall not give it up!" cried Helen almost fiercely, while the slumbering fire of her southern nature flashed into her face. "You have waited so long, worked so hard, suffered so much, you must not lose your reward. You promised, and you must keep the promise."

"But it is so beautiful, so noble to forgive, and return a blessing for a curse. Let us bury the old feud, and right the old wrong in a new way. Those two are so blameless, it is cruel to visit the sins of the dead on their innocent heads. My lady has suffered enough already, and Lillian is so young, so happy, so unfit to meet a storm like this. Oh, Helen, mercy is more divine than justice."

Something moved Paul deeply, and Helen seemed about to yield, when the name of Lillian wrought a subtle change in her. The color died out of her face, her black eyes burned with a gloomy fire, and her voice was relentless as she answered, while her frail hands held him fast, "I will not let you give it up. We are as innocent as they; we have suffered more; and we deserve our rights, for we have no sin to expiate. Go on, Paul, and forget the sentimental folly that unmans you."

Something in her words seemed to sting or wound him. His face darkened, and he put her away, saying briefly, "Let it be so then. In an hour we must go."

On the evening of the same day, Lady Trevlyn and her daughter sat together in the octagon room at the Hall. Twilight was falling and candles were not yet brought, but a cheery fire blazed in the wide chimney, filling the apartment with a ruddy glow, turning Lillian's bright hair to gold and lending a tinge of color to my lady's pallid cheeks. The girl sat on a low lounging chair before the fire, her head on her hand, her eyes on the red embers, her thoughts—where? My lady lay on her couch, a little in the shadow, regarding her daughter with an anxious air, for over the young face a somber change had passed which filled her with disquiet.

"You are out of spirits, love," she said at last, breaking the long silence, as Lillian gave an unconscious sigh and leaned wearily into the depths of her chair.

"Yes, Mamma, a little."

"What is it? Are you ill?"

"No, Mamma; I think London gaiety is rather too much for me. I'm too young for it, as you often say, and I've found it out."

"Then it is only weariness that makes you so pale and grave, and so bent on coming back here?"

Lillian was the soul of truth, and with a moment's hesitation answered slowly, "Not that alone, Mamma. I'm worried about other things. Don't ask me what, please."

"But I must ask. Tell me, child, what things? Have you seen any one? Had letters, or been annoyed in any way about—anything?"

My lady spoke with sudden energy and rose on her arm, eyeing the girl with unmistakable suspicion and excitement.

"No, Mamma, it's only a foolish trouble of my own," answered Lillian, with a glance of surprise and a shamefaced look as the words reluctantly left her lips.

"Ah, a love trouble, nothing more? Thank God for that!" And my lady sank back as if a load was off her mind. "Tell me all, my darling; there is no confidante like a mother."

"You are very kind, and perhaps you can cure my folly if I tell it, and yet I am ashamed," murmured the girl. Then yielding to an irresistible impulse to ask help and sympathy, she added, in an almost inaudible tone, "I came away to escape from Paul."

"Because he loves you, Lillian?" asked my lady, with a frown and a half smile.

"Because he does *not* love me, Mamma." And the poor girl hid her burning cheeks in her hands, as if overwhelmed with maidenly shame at the implied confession of her own affection.

"My child, how is this? I cannot but be glad that he does *not* love you; yet it fills me with grief to see that this pains you. He is not a mate for you, Lillian. Remember this, and forget the transient regard that has sprung up from that early intimacy of yours."

"He is wellborn, and now my equal in fortune, and oh, so much my superior in all gifts of mind and heart," sighed the girl, still with hidden face, for tears were dropping through her slender fingers.

"It may be, but there is a mystery about him; and I have a vague dislike to him in spite of all that has passed. But, darling, are you sure he does not care for you? I fancied I read a different story in his face, and when you begged to leave town so suddenly, I believed that you had seen this also, and kindly wished to spare him any pain."

"It was to spare myself. Oh, Mamma, he loves Helen, and will marry her although she is blind. He told me this, with a look I could not doubt, and so I came away to hide my sorrow," sobbed poor Lillian in despair.

Lady Trevlyn went to her and, laying the bright head on her motherly bosom, said soothingly as she caressed it, "My little girl, it is too soon for you to know these troubles, and I am punished for yielding to your entreaties for a peep at the gay world. It is now too late to spare you this; you have had your wish and must pay its price, dear. But, Lillian, call pride to aid you, and conquer this fruitless love. It cannot be very deep as yet, for you have known Paul, the man, too short a time to be hopelessly enamored. Remember, there are others, better, braver, more worthy of you; that life is long, and full of pleasure yet untried."

"Have no fears for me, Mamma. I'll not disgrace you or myself by any sentimental folly. I do love Paul, but I can conquer it, and I will. Give me a little time, and you shall see me quite myself again."

Lillian lifted her head with an air of proud resolve that satisfied her mother, and with a grateful kiss stole away to ease her full heart alone. As she disappeared Lady Trevlyn drew a long breath and, clasping her hands with a gesture of thanksgiving, murmured to herself in an accent of relief, "Only a love sorrow! I feared it was some new terror like the old one. Seventeen years of silence, seventeen years of secret dread and remorse for me," she said, pacing the room with tightly locked hands and eyes full of unspeakable anguish. "Oh, Richard, Richard! I forgave you long ago, and surely I have expiated my innocent offense by these years of suffering! For her sake I did it, and for her sake I still keep dumb. God knows I ask nothing for myself but rest and oblivion by your side."

Half an hour later, Paul stood at the hall door. It was ajar, for the family had returned unexpectedly, as was evident from the open doors and empty halls. Entering unseen, he ascended to the room my lady usually occupied. The fire burned low, Lillian's chair was empty, and my lady lay asleep, as if lulled by the sighing winds without and the deep silence that reigned within. Paul stood regarding her with a great pity softening his face as he marked the sunken eyes, pallid cheeks, locks too early gray, and restless lips muttering in dreams.

"I wish I could spare her this," he sighed, stooping to wake her with a word. But he did not speak, for, suddenly clutching the chain about her neck, she seemed to struggle with some invisible foe and beat it off, muttering audibly as she clenched her thin hands on the golden case. Paul leaned and listened as if the first word had turned him to stone, till the paroxysm had passed, and with a heavy sigh my lady sank into a calmer sleep. Then, with a quick glance over his shoulder, Paul skillfully opened the locket, drew out the silver key, replaced it with one from the piano close by, and stole from the house noiselessly as he had entered it.

That night, in the darkest hour before the dawn, a figure went gliding through the shadowy Park to its most solitary corner. Here stood the tomb of the Trevlyns, and here the figure paused. A dull spark of light woke in its hand, there was a clank of bars, the creak of rusty hinges, then light and figure both seemed swallowed up.

Standing in the tomb where the air was close and heavy, the pale glimmer of the lantern showed piles of moldering coffins in the niches, and everywhere lay tokens of decay and death. The man drew his hat lower over his eyes, pulled the muffler closer about his mouth, and surveyed the spot with an undaunted aspect, though the beating of his heart was heard in the deep silence. Nearest the door stood a long casket covered with black velvet and richly decorated with silver ornaments, tarnished now. The Trevlyns had been a stalwart race, and the last sleeper brought there had evidently been of goodly stature, for the modern coffin was as ponderous as the great oaken beds where lay the bones of generations. Lifting the lantern, the intruder brushed the dust from the shield-shaped plate, read the name RICHARD TREVLYN and a date, and, as if satisfied, placed a key in the lock, half-raised the lid, and, averting his head that he might not see the ruin seventeen long years had made, he laid his hand on the dead breast and from the folded shroud drew a mildewed paper. One glance sufficed, the casket was relocked, the door rebarred, the light extinguished, and the man vanished like a ghost in the darkness of the wild October night.

VIII

WHICH?

A Gentleman, my lady."

Taking a card from the silver salver on which the servant offered it, Lady Trevlyn read, "Paul Talbot," and below the name these penciled words, "I beseech you to see me." Lillian stood beside her and saw the line. Their eyes met, and in the girl's face was such a sudden glow of hope, and love, and longing, that the mother could not doubt or disappoint her wish.

"I will see him," she said.

"Oh, Mamma, how kind you are!" cried the girl with a passionate embrace, adding breathlessly, "He did not ask for me. I cannot see him yet. I'll hide in the alcove, and can appear or run away as I like when we know why he comes."

They were in the library, for, knowing Lillian's fondness for the room which held no dark memories for her, my lady conquered her dislike and often sat there. As she spoke, the girl glided into the deep recess of a bay window and drew the heavy curtains just as Paul's step sounded at the door.

Hiding her agitation with a woman's skill, my lady rose with outstretched hand to welcome him. He bowed but did not take the hand, saying, in a voice of grave respect in which was audible an undertone of strong emotion, "Pardon me, Lady Trevlyn. Hear what I have to say; and then if you offer me your hand, I shall gratefully receive it."

She glanced at him, and saw that he was very pale, that his eye glittered with suppressed excitement, and his whole manner was that of a man who had nerved himself up to the performance of a difficult but intensely interesting task. Fancying these signs of agitation only natural in a young lover coming to woo, my lady smiled, reseated herself, and calmly answered, "I will listen patiently. Speak freely, Paul, and remember I am an old friend."

"I wish I could forget it. Then my task would be easier," he murmured in a voice of mingled regret and resolution, as he leaned on a tall chair opposite and wiped his damp forehead, with a look of such deep compassion that her heart sank with a nameless fear.

"I must tell you a long story, and ask your forgiveness for the offenses I committed against you when a boy. A mistaken sense of duty guided me, and I obeyed it blindly. Now I see my error and regret it," he said earnestly.

"Go on," replied my lady, while the vague dread grew stronger, and she braced her nerves as for some approaching shock. She forgot Lillian, forgot everything but the strange aspect of the man before her, and the words to which she listened like a statue. Still standing pale and steady, Paul spoke rapidly, while his eyes were full of mingled sternness, pity, and remorse.

"Twenty years ago, an English gentleman met a friend in a little Italian town, where he had married a beautiful wife. The wife had a sister as lovely as herself, and the young man, during that brief stay, loved and married her—in a very private manner, lest his father should disinherit him. A few months passed, and the Englishman was called home to take possession of his title and estates, the father being dead. He went alone, promising to send for the wife when all was ready. He told no one of his marriage, meaning to surprise his English friends by producing the lovely woman unexpectedly. He had been in England but a short time when he received a letter from the old priest of the Italian town, saying the cholera had swept through it, carrying off half its inhabitants, his wife and friend among others. This blow prostrated the young man, and when he recovered he hid his grief, shut himself up in his country house, and tried to forget. Accident threw in his way another lovely woman, and he married again. Before the first year was out, the friend whom he supposed was dead appeared, and told him that his wife still lived, and had borne him a child. In the terror and confusion of the plague, the priest had mistaken one sister for the other, as the elder did die."

"Yes, yes, I know; go on!" gasped my lady, with white lips, and eyes that never left the narrator's face.

"This friend had met with misfortune after flying from the doomed village with the surviving sister. They had waited long for letters, had written, and, when no answer came, had been delayed by illness and poverty from reaching England. At this time the child was born, and the friend, urged by the wife and his own interest, came here, learned that Sir Richard was married, and hurried to him in much distress. We can imagine the grief and horror of the unhappy man. In that interview the friend promised to leave all to Sir Richard, to preserve the secret till some means of relief could be found; and with this promise he returned, to guard and comfort the forsaken wife. Sir Richard wrote the truth to Lady Trevlyn, meaning to kill himself, as the only way of escape from the terrible situation between two women, both so beloved, both so innocently wronged. The pistol lay ready, but death came without its aid, and Sir Richard was spared the sin of suicide."

Paul paused for breath, but Lady Trevlyn motioned him to go on, still sitting rigid and white as the marble image near her.

"The friend only lived to reach home and tell the story. It killed the wife, and she died, imploring the old priest to see her child righted and its father's name secured to it. He promised; but he was poor, the child was a frail baby, and he waited. Years passed, and when the child was old enough to ask for its parents and demand its due, the proofs of the marriage were lost, and nothing remained but a ring, a bit of writing, and the name. The priest was very old, had neither friends, money, nor proofs to help him; but I was strong and hopeful, and though a mere boy I resolved to do the work. I made my way to England, to Trevlyn Hall, and by various stratagems (among which, I am ashamed to say, were false keys and feigned sleepwalking) I collected many proofs, but nothing which would satisfy a court, for no one but you knew where Sir Richard's confession was. I searched every nook and corner of the Hall, but in vain, and began to despair, when news of the death of Father Cosmo recalled me to Italy; for Helen was left to my care then. The old man had faithfully recorded the facts and left witnesses to prove the truth of his story; but for four years I never used it, never made any effort to secure the title or estates."

"Why not?" breathed my lady in a faint whisper, as hope suddenly revived.

"Because I was grateful," and for the first time Paul's voice faltered. "I was a stranger, and you took me in. I never could forget that, nor tie many kindnesses bestowed upon the friendless boy. This afflicted me, even while I was acting a false part, and when I was away my heart failed me. But Helen gave me no peace; for my sake, she urged me to keep the vow made to that poor mother, and threatened to tell the story herself. Talbot's benefaction left me no excuse for delaying longer, and I came to finish the hardest task I can ever undertake. I feared that a long dispute would follow any appeal to law, and meant to appeal first to you, but fate befriended me, and the last proof was found."

"Found! Where?" cried Lady Trevlyn, springing up aghast.

　　　　　　　　　　　　　　　　　　LOUISA MAY ALCOTT

"In Sir Richard's coffin, where you hid it, not daring to destroy, yet fearing to keep it."

"Who has betrayed me?" And her eye glanced wildly about the room, as if she feared to see some spectral accuser.

"Your own lips, my lady. Last night I came to speak of this. You lay asleep, and in some troubled dream spoke of the paper, safe in its writer's keeping, and your strange treasure here, the key of which you guarded day and night. I divined the truth. Remembering Hester's stories, I took the key from your helpless hand, found the paper on Sir Richard's dead breast, and now demand that you confess your part in this tragedy."

"I do, I do! I confess, I yield, I relinquish everything, and ask pity only for my child."

Lady Trevlyn fell upon her knees before him, with a submissive gesture, but imploring eyes, for, amid the wreck of womanly pride and worldly fortune, the mother's heart still clung to its idol.

"Who should pity her, if not I? God knows I would have spared her this blow if I could; but Helen would not keep silent, and I was driven to finish what I had begun. Tell Lillian this, and do not let her hate me."

As Paul spoke, tenderly, eagerly, the curtain parted, and Lillian appeared, trembling with the excitement of that interview, but conscious of only one emotion as she threw herself into his arms, crying in a tone of passionate delight, "Brother! Brother! Now I may love you!"

Paul held her close, and for a moment forgot everything but the joy of that moment. Lillian spoke first, looking up through tears of tenderness, her little hand laid caressingly against his cheek, as she whispered with sudden bloom in her own, "Now I know why I loved you so well, and now I can see you marry Helen without breaking my heart. Oh, Paul, you are still mine, and I care for nothing else."

"But, Lillian, I am not your brother."

"Then, in heaven's name, who are you?" she cried, tearing herself from his arms.

"Your lover, dear!"

"Who, then, is the heir?" demanded Lady Trevlyn, springing up, as Lillian turned to seek shelter with her mother.

"I am."

Helen spoke, and Helen stood on the threshold of the door, with a hard, haughty look upon her beautiful face.

"You told your story badly, Paul," she said, in a bitter tone. "You forgot me, forgot my affliction, my loneliness, my wrongs, and the natural desire of a child to clear her mother's honor and claim her father's name. I am Sir Richard's eldest daughter. I can prove my birth, and I demand my right with his own words to sustain me."

She paused, but no one spoke; and with a slight tremor in her proud voice, she added, "Paul has done the work; he shall have the reward. I only want my father's name. Title and fortune are nothing to one like me. I coveted and claimed them that I might give them to you, Paul, my one friend, always, so tender and so true."

"I'll have none of it," he answered, almost fiercely. "I have kept my promise, and am free. You chose to claim your own, although I offered all I had to buy your silence. It is yours by right—take it, and enjoy it if you can. I'll have no reward for work like this."

He turned from her with a look that would have stricken her to the heart could she have seen it. She felt it, and it seemed to augment some secret anguish, for she pressed her hands against her bosom with an expression of deep suffering, exclaiming passionately, "Yes, I *will* keep it, since I am to lose all else. I am tired of pity. Power is sweet, and I will use it. Go, Paul, and be happy if you can, with a nameless wife, and the world's compassion or contempt to sting your pride."

"Oh, Lillian, where shall we go? This is no longer our home, but who will receive us now?" cried Lady Trevlyn, in a tone of despair, for her spirit was utterly broken by the thought of the shame and sorrow in store for this beloved and innocent child.

"I will." And Paul's face shone with a love and loyalty they could not doubt. "My lady, you gave me a home when I was homeless; now let me pay my debt. Lillian, I have loved you from the time when, a romantic boy, I wore your little picture in my breast, and vowed to win you if I lived. I dared not speak before, but now, when other hearts may be shut against you, mine stands wide open to welcome you. Come, both. Let me protect and cherish you, and so atone for the sorrow I have brought you."

It was impossible to resist the sincere urgency of his voice, the tender reverence of his manner, as he took the two forlorn yet innocent creatures into the shelter of his strength and love. They clung to him instinctively, feeling that there still remained to them one staunch friend whom adversity could not estrange.

An eloquent silence fell upon the room, broken only by sobs, grateful whispers, and the voiceless vows that lovers plight with eyes, and hands, and tender lips. Helen was forgotten, till Lillian, whose elastic spirit threw off sorrow as a flower sheds the rain, looked up to

LOUISA MAY ALCOTT

thank Paul, with smiles as well as tears, and saw the lonely figure in the shadow. Her attitude was full of pathetic significance; she still stood on the threshold, for no one had welcomed her, and in the strange room she knew not where to go; her hands were clasped before her face, as if those sightless eyes had seen the joy she could not share, and at her feet lay the time-stained paper that gave her a barren title, but no love. Had Lillian known how sharp a conflict between passion and pride, jealousy and generosity, was going on in that young heart, she could not have spoken in a tone of truer pity or sincerer goodwill than that in which she softly said, "Poor girl! We must not forget her, for, with all her wealth, she is poor compared to us. We both had one father, and should love each other in spite of this misfortune. Helen, may I call you sister?"

"Not yet. Wait till I deserve it."

As if that sweet voice had kindled an answering spark of nobleness in her own heart, Helen's face changed beautifully, as she tore the paper to shreds, saying in a glad, impetuous tone, while the white flakes fluttered from her hands, "I, too, can be generous. I, too, can forgive. I bury the sad past. See! I yield my claim, I destroy my proofs, I promise eternal silence, and keep 'Paul's cousin' for my only title. Yes, you are happy, for you love one another!" she cried, with a sudden passion of tears. "Oh, forgive me, pity me, and take me in, for I am all alone and in the dark!"

There could be but one reply to an appeal like that, and they gave it, as they welcomed her with words that sealed a household league of mutual secrecy and sacrifice.

They *were* happy, for the world never knew the hidden tie that bound them so faithfully together, never learned how well the old prophecy had been fulfilled, or guessed what a tragedy of life and death the silver key unlocked.

A Note About the Author

Louisa May Alcott (1832–1888) was an American novelist, poet, and short story writer. Born in Philadelphia to a family of transcendentalists—her parents were friends with Ralph Waldo Emerson, Nathaniel Hawthorne, and Henry David Thoreau—Alcott was raised in Massachusetts. She worked from a young age as a teacher, seamstress, and domestic worker in order to alleviate her family's difficult financial situation. These experiences helped to guide her as a professional writer, just as her family's background in education reform, social work, and abolition—their home was a safe house for escaped slaves on the Underground Railroad—aided her development as an early feminist and staunch abolitionist. Her career began as a writer for the *Atlantic Monthly* in 1860, took a brief pause while she served as a nurse in a Georgetown Hospital for wounded Union soldiers during the Civil War, and truly flourished with the 1868 and 1869 publications of parts one and two of *Little Women*. The first installment of her acclaimed and immensely popular "March Family Saga" has since become a classic of American literature and has been adapted countless times for the theater, film, and television. Alcott was a prolific writer throughout her lifetime, with dozens of novels, short stories, and novelettes published under her name, as the pseudonym *a.m.* Barnard, and anonymously.

A Note from the Publisher

Spanning many genres, from non-fiction essays to literature classics to children's books and lyric poetry, Mint Edition books showcase the master works of our time in a modern new package. The text is freshly typeset, is clean and easy to read, and features a new note about the author in each volume. Many books also include exclusive new introductory material. Every book boasts a striking new cover, which makes it as appropriate for collecting as it is for gift giving. Mint Edition books are only printed when a reader orders them, so natural resources are not wasted. We're proud that our books are never manufactured in excess and exist only in the exact quantity they need to be read and enjoyed. To learn more and view our library, go to minteditionbooks.com

CPSIA information can be obtained
at www.ICGtesting.com
Printed in the USA
LVHW081801060521
686702LV00013B/1748

9 781513 280080